*A wayfaring physician attends to a local merchant
on the road to the Andalusian Plains, 1432*

SARDINE CAN'T

Jim Bell

ISBN: 978-0-6480946-8-5

www.jbellstories.com

to the old day star
the busted moon
the seesawn seas
& she

CONTENTS

RIVER ODD..3

IN TOO TOWN...4

LOVE YARD 7

THE SIBYL AND THE SAINT.......................9

LOSTRALIA 15

NO VISAS
FOR THEIR BAGGY SOULS 17

FROM OUT THE DARK NIGHT
OF THE CIRCUMSCRIBED I.......................19

THE OLD MEN OF THE SEA 23

DAY OF JOANNE..27

THE FARE OF BATS.....................................33

LOVING GHOSTS 37

FICKLE DEEDS AND
MODERN CRIMES..38

FORLORN DREAM 41

THE SURVEILLANTS...................................42

LONE APPARATCHIKS
TOSSING STONES..45

HELL'N..48

THE REGIONAL MAYOR 49

15 BIRDS DREAM 52

THE LEPERS OF FORTINBRAS 53

HE WHO LAUGHS WITH THE CROW 59

DONNA UNPLUGGED 62

THAT ODD ID 64

THIS DYSLEXIC DRANG 67

WAR DREAM (France, 1944) 69

BETTER RED THAN WED 71

SEQUELAE 73

HOONIO AND IOLA.....................................74

HOG HEAVEN 77

FILCHER...82

THAT OLD FACTORY DREAM....................83

VINCE...84

FLOSSING RIBS
SO THE HEART MIGHT SEE 87

CREASE OF A WING 93

FRIEND OR FIEND DREAM.......................94

AND THE DEAD SHEEP
WASH UP ON SHORE 95

THE ENDING DAY.......................................100

THE HEART IS A GORGON 101

MAGGOT DAWN MANNA 104

A SCALPEL IN THE TOSS
AS BALLOONS FLOAT ABOUT 107

DRAG ME, AIM ME 108

THE SCRUBBING END 111

TO ASSESS THE SINS
OF ALL ASSASSINS 113

A SUCCUBUS SNEERS
ON A BROKEN MAN'S BACK
AS HE SNORES 119

EVERYTHING STARTS
WITH A STING 120

LOST IN THE RUBBLE 122

SKINT ON SKINS..123

ENFRANCHISED PARVIS 135

DIASTOLE AND SYSTOLE 137

THE WEDDING AXE 139

ANGEL IN THE AIRPORT 148

LATE REQUIEM
FOR A BYSTANDER 150

SARDINE CAN'T

RIVER ODD

The stew that binds everything together,
such as the lunch you feed
the sparrows every day,
makes the world complete . . .

The old and the new
are the same.
The lack of . . .
The lot of . . .
The have and not-have . . .
The same old game of eld . . .

Take it as an ant carries crumbs.
Treasure it like a dog's bone.
The world has only ever served
servants within worlds . . .

IN TOO TOWN

Seeing a dog chase a wind
carrying the 18 feet of G-d behind it
is a sure-fire sign
that the drugs have kicked in
more than hoped for . . .

Jock went *"What?"*
when Surita turned around to him,
& his head swung around the same
to her,
just like in that old jumble sale mirror ad
they once saw
& always laughed about . . .

Surita was soon lying at his feet
— tongue out, wheezing up
at the sky again.

4

"Did you see that wind? she said.

"They were the feet of G-d," Jock said.

"And the dog was death," she snapped,
"like all dead dogs."

Later, she vomited,
& then they went back to bed,
& napped again.
After a while,
Jock looked down at his knees
as if they weren't there,
& there she was:
"Are you sure?""
he said loudly to her,
half-asleep . . .

Surita slowly dragged her lips
up the length
of the long scar on his leg
& said back to his guts: *"Yeah."*
Then she got up to get dressed . . .

"We need milk," he slurred.

But she didn't say anything back.
He soon went to work as well . . .

Inside the baker's
he just sat there,
like a billion other smiling liars
at nine o'clock,
Monday morning . . .

It soon comes through
the leather in the seats;
the shit fear of death.
It comes out through the pores
in the back of hands
as well . . .

Jock saw it on the face
of somebody dead once;
fingerprints in flour
right round her throat.
Famed baker of the coast.
He knew who was the first one to hate.
Surita had an eye for retrograde
in any case.
"It doesn't matter," they all say at first.
Afterwards, it's all a lie.
At least that's what
he used to think . . .

LOVE YARD

They can all sense the used love.
How it's been ransacked
a million times
& thrown back in his face.
When they squint,
they can all still see the faint stains,
where time and again,
he'd peeled if off
like a tossed octopus
that nearly asphyxiated him
as it wrapped
all its deadly legs
around his life . . .

They can all only disavow
such messes now.
Like the way
all accidentally trod
in a tamed creature's stools
across the threshold.
They can all still only see
the same meanderings
of their time
as ill-conceived that first hour,
as when first,

they too had taken refuge
in the initial solace of another . . .

And their own hearts now?
Only a quart away from teeming, too,
before joining
the same clan as all,
hobbling along
with the same blemish,
instigating horror in the passing faces,
long years away
from ever even seeing
what stains of love truly are,
or what even unused love
really is . . .

And what soon will become
of all that
they all so instinctively promote
to be ceremoniously stated
as one? . . .

But time flies
& at the closing hour
nothing is ever redressed
or dourly gambled on
again . . .

THE SIBYL AND THE SAINT

By stormy Gruel Point,
at the mouth of the River Scree,
languished an old Dominican rest home
for tubercular girls.
On a pedestal out front
in the courtyard
stood a greening, copper statue
in scale
of the Blessed Saint Zeema,
with an arm held high,
pointing straight to the heavens . . .

In gentle repose,
a newborn, black butterfly
with tattooed, wine-winked eyes
perched itself
on his wiry apple,
just below
his blubbery bee-stung lips,
& rested . . .

Zeema was once a famed raconteur
of the faith,
who had helped conquer
the distant battlefields

of the Levant,
& who had passed away
at the behest of a foreign land's
hasty horse lice in transit . . .

Affectionately chiseled
in immaculate granite,
beneath his auk-shatted,
strapped soldier boots,
was a restored copperplate inscription
in Tartarean black
of a misquoted maxim
he once drunkenly slurred
in the company of his allies
when trying to seize upon the means
to outwit
their worst adversary:
"A fart (sic) cannot be blamed
for suspecting our judgement
in matters of religion."
["Fact" was never an agent
of his barleyed vocabulary.]

In his wild adolescent years
on the other side of the world
he was even then
seen by all as
— floridly —

a belated soldier of prophecy,
who regularly entertained
all those in the lower strata,
& was soon adopted
as one of their own
by even those more diehard snipers
on the fringes of every colony . . .

After his many infamous
skirmishes in the fields
with his opponents,
Zeema would often charge
straight back from the trenches
to the stage,
rambling scripture
to yet another mob
hooked on vengeance
— all the old heirs
of the trophy brigades
from earlier wars,
& all the grieving collaborationists
in stumbled conference —
who were always openly pining
for true religious fervor
to ripen,
so that all their convenient dogmas
could be fully exploited
when unbottled . . .

A few generations before
Zeema's time,
a leprous but priestly woman
tagged "*Gangrenous Natalie,*"
who regularly set out
each dawn
in her seaweed camouflage suit
to the vista of the shore,
(to snare mutton birds
for her progeny)
was the first to suspect
that a saviour in prophecy
— with pointed finger to the sky —
would come to the shire
as a divine commander . . .

Natalie discovered this sign
one morning
in the gloaming,
whilst hidden to one side
of her quarry
in the burrows,
holding a dozen twines in one hand,
& browsing the margins
of her mother's star chart,
when suddenly she spotted
a malefic stellium
in synch with her tuitions . . .

She soon heralded to all
those hedonists
across the peninsula
of the "*brilliance warp*"
she'd stumbled upon,
espousing joyously
of her certainty that soon
this saviour would settle
amongst their debauched throng
and drunken constituency . . .

But,
to her surprise,
she was damned as a blasphemer,
& they banished her
without regard
to the battered-out ruins
of Gurney Prison
on the edge of town,
imbuing her
with the full recognition
of that feeble truth
that only justice is man-made;
& through the cell grate
above her
she could hear the cane scaffolding
being assembled
for her heretic end . . .

On her last day alive,
she could hear in back
the approaching drumming din
of the Execution Marching Band,
drunkenly blowing their dirges
on old conches,
& braying wildly of her demise,
all in lieu of losing
the hallowed effects
of their specious culture
& race . . .

The join-in chorus
of the decadent crowd
eating into her mind,
treating her end as just a carnival;
blindly celebratory,
like a dinner's gong . . .

"We want just and able lovers,
and joyous tales and song;
the wildest of concoctions,
all day and all night long!"

LOSTRALIA

At the tail end of its time,
one island became heavier,
& before long,
still,
with its new weight supported,
it became lighter
— in shade.

Far from bonding
with intricate colour,
this new ballast
began to chip & slash,
till the obstinate, stubborn
fixation crumbled,
evaporating into the air,

seeping into the land,
taking with it
in a sad journey
the reflection of a white dial
with reddened eyes . . .

And like a kerchief
dropped over a hole,
this white spread far
& wide,
educating offspring
to trampoline
on the nose-rag
covering the well;
& with all the hick skills
of the pirates of history
the four corners of this rag
were un-aggrievedly pegged down,
sealing
sealing
SEALING
SEALING
the seams
of the rejected pit . . .

NO VISAS
FOR THEIR BAGGY SOULS

If the world can abide,
but always bid
the parting quick,
so that all of a din
can seal a time
as an end,
what comes of all
the belated lulls of silence?

Or are all these
just dreams instead?

Are lily pads the sponges of night?
What lies curl dry
off a wishing-well's wall?
If only the hours were horses
& not sloven nags . . .

But the drunken clouds roll in,
& every petal in flux
signals to the thrips
the last gleaned breath
of nature's dirty threat . . .

If the fish
& the worm
can steal through this mess,
& the eagle
& the bat
can tilt by
free as kites
across its wreck,
when will this tilled ball of muck
submit a true bonanza
for the rest;
or is this forever,
on our behalf,
just a test?

FROM OUT THE DARK NIGHT
OF THE CIRCUMSCRIBED I

There was an odd scenario
that would sometimes unfold
when working in retail
that used to tear Stash apart.
He'd start serving a woman
he'd just met,
whom he immediately liked,
& then
— within seconds
of looking into her eyes —
she'd somehow worm
her *"boyfriend"*
or *"husband"* into the mix,
just to put him off . . .

It always used to turn
his old lonely guts over
like a grave,
realising he'd been apparent
in his desire for her,
and that she had to take
a certain step
to quickly steer him away . . .

No matter how he'd try to disguise
his even subtlest interest in someone,
he was beginning to suspect
he was giving himself
all too easily away;
because he always felt
he was never able to mount
any sort of defense with someone
he thought he liked.
You'd get what you'd see with Stash;
but nobody seemed to
ever want to take it up . . .

It seemed to happen
with almost every woman
he'd meet of late.
But when they'd mention their partner,
he'd try to muster up
some composure,
as if it really meant nothing to him;
when, *clearly,*
it was only then
that he cut eye contact with them,
unable to squarely give of himself
anymore,
though he'd keep on talking
as if nothing horrible had just unfolded
inside his heart . . .

And though they could always see
that he was hurt,
it didn't ever seem to matter
too much to them.
He'd finally leave for home,
as if everything was intact within,
then berate himself for days,
succumbing to the old sadnesses again,
evermore sure
that he was utterly nothing . . .

But for some reason,
he's found of late
that's it's really all amusing
in the end
— the way they all just do it.
It just happened again today,
& he nearly laughed out loud
when she mentioned her other half
in Zabriskie Point
within seconds of talking with her.
And in a way, he's glad now
that she said it,
because now he knows
where he stands,
& he won't think of her anymore,
which is — he supposes —
why she did it . . .

But it was strange when she left him.
He didn't berate himself at all,
like all those times before,
& he didn't succumb
to the old sadnesses again.
It made its initial sting;
but something inside himself
pushed him to override it,
knowing it was just a pain
he couldn't afford to taste anymore.
And it didn't hurt so much as before.
Then he suddenly realised
that maybe he was finally
learning something,
& he seemed relieved about that;
though he wasn't exactly sure
what that lesson was . . .

He's tempted to try it again
with someone else now,
as soon as he can,
just to see if they'll do it;
because he's sure
he'll just laugh his head off now,
roaring himself
back into purity . . .

[Title from a line in a Leon Trotsky essay, 1935]

THE OLD MEN OF THE SEA

The old men
slowly shuffle to shore
& drop their bundles
on the sand
close to sea . . .

They're all usually emaciated,
with great balding shell-shocked
heads of war,
& they're always alone,
& they always pick
a somewhat secluded spot,
though not too far
from anyone else,
& particularly youth . . .

They drop their old dungarees
to the sand
& slowly strip down
to their jungle shorts,
exposing wracked, tattooed carcasses
that have withstood
the pangs
of the world's most gruelling
crusades . . .

And they make not a sound,
look to nowhere
but their own gangly toes,
& they slowly step into the shallows,
with the set determination of soldiers,
& dive in
to pleasantly disappear . . .

And everybody else on the beach
forgets about them,
& in the air can be heard
the whoops of brats riddled with joy
& all the cooing mothers,
squatted on towels,
rubbing creams
into their children's pores . . .

And further back
— like at the back seats of buses —
lie the circles of bathing youths
on their ribs,
all with shiny, wet hair,
sniggering to each other . . .

And the little flocks of gulls
at attention nearby,
always squawking their battle-cries,
but always mistaking cigarettes
for fare . . .

Then suddenly the old men
are seen again,
swimming across the surface of the sea,
lifting their shell-shocked heads of war
side to side
for gulps of air,
pounding their withered, tattooed arms
with unexpected strength
into the water,
smoothly scooping themselves along
like unwinding toy boats,
all so gentle
& full of grace;
then they glide to a stop like otters,
all alone,
& turn back again
— always hugging close to shore
in case of attack —
endlessly swimming back
& forth
across the aprons
of the lagoons . . .

And then they suddenly cease,
with only their great
shell-shocked heads of war
poking out of the sea,
staring expressionless

to the unbroken line of the horizon,
& they each always calmly breathe
with relief again,
then swim on once more . . .
(Habit-memory of the war.)

And everyone on the beach
secretively watches on
with admiration,
amazed at their calm
& grace,
admiring everything about them;
but they soon attend
to their broods again,
putting on second coats of cream,
passing out drinks
& salad rolls,
& by the time they look back out
to the old man of the sea,
he's long left the water unseen,
dried himself off
with his flannelette towel,
pulled his dungarees back on,
picked up his bundle from the sand
& disappeared again
back into his anonymous life.
If there were issued medals
for such poignant frolics . . .

DAY OF JOANNE

"Wonderful day!" she thinks,
or *"Disastrous day!"*
or sometimes
"Glorious day!"
or it's
"The weirdest day!"
as she scrambles down
the lanes of town
with a just-penned letter
in hand
— Ah, the pssst in post!

All the locals are restless.
All the straggling pensioners
& petitioners are out
on *"pay day,"*
misfitting around
the country streets,
with the Rabelaisian fear
of being rubbed to death
by geese,
bristling up
the whitened hairs
on each their wringing
necks . . .

Happy to the psychopathy,
she heads back home
along the dusty country road,
watching the El Nino effects
of the clouds,
& the deft work of quolls,
listening to the flies
buzzing their aches,
laughing at all the cattle in kilts
stuck grievously to their grasses,
staring up at rickety carts
passing by
like starving cats espying doves,
& seeing little she,
Joanne,
as Auto-girl frolicking past,
before the long slumber
of their dreamless kip
kicks in . . .

All of them
soon snoring on their hooves,
still gassing
the giant black sky in their sleep,
& she and her siblings
sneaking through the wire fences
& pushing them all over
in the dark

those quiet deadly eves,
& watching them
slide down the glens
& the thick, muddied, daffodilled banks
into the icy ponds
with all their endless bubbles
rising to the brim
to make a mooing hellish spring.
They used to pop them
like balloons
with twigs
to wile the country nights! . . .

Nearing the drafty log cabin,
she heard the old shanties
of an ancient voice inside,
"In my eyes are 13 sloths
dying of malnutrition!"
& some raucous sea-dog gag
about the *"Voracious gorging*
of gorgonzolan pies!"
& much hearty guffaw all round . . .

Just as she stepped inside
with her brothers
— they'd all just finished
splitting kindling by the shed —
she heard:

"Good night un-abortioned!
Uncle Funster is home!"
in his mock-Hollywood Christ air
to her twin sisters
gurgling in the bassinet
in the corner,
& her parents laughing crazy . . .

She didn't know
— never knew —
what he ever meant . . .

And then he duly commenced
to sell off all his violence
like soap to all,
telling everyone
in a huge ocean voice,
"There are no atheists in foxholes!"
as he sprinkled grilled gar
with other assorted pablums
& wisps . . .

"They're all just id now,"
he sniggered.
"Just all id."

Whatever that meant . . .

Her pop
— his long loyal brother —
the other weatherbeaten doll
of her likeness,
was soon vehemently raving of the
*"Rump government archetypes
ruling all,"*
& questioning the lack
of moral license
in everything ever recently welled . . .

Then someone muttered
"Eleemosynary!"
& someone else said *"Aegis!"*
but those younger
& witless,
sitting askew at a tinier table,
had no idea of what
they *all* ever meant . . .

Bizarre images of eels
& haggis
were the only plums
they could ever pick at
in their psyches,
& even then
they were all overripe
& rotted . . .

Little quips were soon
bandied about
— *"The illusionists
robbed of their luggage!"* —
but none of those young
could ever yield
to the maze
all their dying
jingoisms . . .

Joanne thought she'd ask
her pen-friend
in the next round
whether she knew what
any of these words
might mean . . .

Just the smell of frying fish
lingered in the air,
& the eucalypts outside
in ambush
gently wafting by
in the moonlight . . .

THE FARE OF BATS

The Ethiopians weakly point out
how all we ever do is
"Consume,
be silent,
and die,"
whilst they all starve,
screaming to live . . .

It's true.
They stagger ragged night
& ravaged day,
slurping sewerage from ponds,
in the simple search
for sustenance,
whilst Westly
— & maniacally —
we post
& pre-prandially
gorge in slobbering rows
with unmitigated gall
at everything
without even
the slightest tinge
of concern . . .

Forever less affected
to the aches
of a more substantial spell
— as unredeemed
by all those more aggrieved —
we gamble nothing
but our sheer wastes of breath!

Simply nursed by only
the rejuvenating clouds scuttling by,
they resume their rendered airs
less fickle to the gruel
forever apportioned them;
whilst deep down in sack-time,
we murder our own
already mangled claims
for the sorry sake of replenishing
the dwindling reserves
of our own
long mislaid restorations!

Inside our vain lonely eyes,
we falter along the lines
so haphazardly spun
since our programming;
just to stump
that old mottled ghoul
forever in pursuit

— always trailing,
trailing,
TRAILING —
just waiting for that day
we finally drop,
helpless to all its tiny teeths,
& our final resting holes
— *the royal seat*
of the worm's
countersunk anus!

Funny how, firstly,
they always go straight for the orbs.
A little digging through the lids
& then they think they're home
in the centre of all that
forever seen,
adored
& deplored . . .

Windows to the soul,
they clamour through,
spitting out memories
as they go,
seeking the true essence
tucked far down
at the pit of it all,
still long unabsolved . . .

Ah, it's already gone,
you tireless little crooks.
It's skewering up
to the elements
of the night sky
to be dutifully picked at
by the greedy winds
& the stray sonaric fields
of all those
greedily whizzing along
in the trawl for gnats . . .

Maybe souls appear
as such little bugs themselves
& eternally
all are but simply mistaken prey
to the straying Gothic greed
of so many vampiric pests;
only to be ceremoniously
disgorged
in yet another skin
on the earth
to be spread the same
as originally spent,
as when first come,
as when first
all so gruelly whetted . . .

LOVING GHOSTS

Herod mind,
Rasputined heart;
one septillion soul requited.
Planted dreams
are hard retrieved,
like all the sacrifices . . .

Bunk haunt
of the last kept weight;
a snug bear laid in mud.
Toss & turn
in her phantom shame,
the same old game of love . . .

Nuzzled in the ditch
returned,
another slipped dig and off.
Each hip-hack
reaping deeper down;
darker,
dazed,
& scoffed . . .

FICKLE DEEDS AND
MODERN CRIMES

Deep in the bowels of a letted gully,
in the chilly hinterlands
out back of Brogogomorro,
cringes a small band
of secret half-brothers,
each pigeonholed
with a modern woe . . .

Barry suffers from a *"frenzied realism"*.

Whilst Carry wrestles with
*"a greenish contempt
for external perception"*.

Gary openly pines for the health
of his own *"pre-reflexive cogito"*.

Though Harry
— with indifferent cardiac reflexes —
grapples simultaneously
with his own
*"ortho-sexuality
& ideational fugacity"*.

Save Larry
— stunned by his own
surprise attacks
of *"nose-diving neologisms"* —
Parry reels back
by his own exaggerated
"paranoiac sense of logic".

They each whisper *"Boo!"*
to one another
to pass the time,
as the wild boars
drinking warm creek water
scuttle off
by the fledging glen . . .

Little to know,
that all about them,
from the high edges of the valley
in surround,
the local constabulary
— with posse in tow,
& clubs at hand —
were combing the expanse
in search of them all,
mulling over the knowledge
*"that only bums now
are the ones finding God!"*

The posse was a gang
of local musos
from the shire's municipal band
who were seeking
the six strangers
who'd dared to openly pray
amongst the crowd
at the town square recital,
before meeting back
at the glen again,
in the same old busted ditch
in which
they'd each been conceived
by the same father
from the same town . . .

They were all
of the same mettle
at heart though;
as are nearly all now,
weaned as everyone is
on the same formula at large
these days,
in this old,
but slick age
of empty ironies . . .

FORLORN DREAM

Locked in a cell
by a yard,
near a wire fence,
praying,
she stretches a line of skin
3 ways
between
3 deserted towns . . .

She sees a man in the distance
floating on the river
in parts
— a man of each part of skin to love.
Only to not realise
that each part is not all him;
so that each part
is pined for
in the wrong way
the more she craves . . .

THE SURVEILLANTS

All the beasts of the world
are now tagged . . .

All the albatrosses of the skies
are on radar now,
under the watchful gaze
of air-traffic controllers,
shift by shift . . .

All the snapping turtles of the seas
are being tailed
by scientists in submarines,
homing in on the refractions
of radio-waves
bouncing off their shells . . .

All the climbers to the boughs
are being observed
in their natural habitats
by those hidden nearby
in high camouflaged huts
with their infra-red Kodaks . . .

All the crawlers
scuttling across the deserts
are being slowly tracked
by those in dune-buggies,
waving ultra-sensitive
seismic instruments
along the subtle ululations,
for distinct clues
to the patterns
of their sly migrations . . .

All the beasts of the world
are now tagged,
sending little quick bleeps
to all instruments
about the globe,
for the economic purpose
of stably destroying
their natural environments
in less debilitating fashions
than before,
so as to

— in gradual accruement —
fully counter
the mismanagement
of previous generations,
& reap yet further riches
for the future,
though still at the expense
of those indigenous
to their every quarter . . .

All the shy mouflon
are now fully located in the glens
of the mountaintops . . .

All the quaggas
have been found
in their niches
& crannies . . .

All the iridescent trails of snails
are being monitored
via satellite
each frosty morn
as they make
their slow pilgrimages
to more nutritional foliage . . .

Etc.

LONE APPARATCHIKS
TOSSING STONES

Mobsters are everywhere now,
flogging the meat of mad dogs
as sirloin
to the poorest of suburbs,
with all their Barbies in tow,
now too peeped to pap
on show;
still homesick
for their old hideaway in *"Banff,"*
where everyone just lets loose
their old death wish
at any whim
to be whetted . . .

In their elite, mellow years
they'll soon cherish community,
& join in class actions
to sue prized moguls
for making them *"trigger tears"*
over the years,
just to make a kickback:
*"We have all suffered
under your imaginary tales
of duress for too long!"*

Their lawyers were ruthless.
PC was rife then,
& sweeping the world
just like the bird flu.
Soon, no one could bear talking
to anyone anymore
for the fear of saying something wrong.
Cinemas & stadiums
were shutting down everywhere
because people
just didn't seem to like people anymore,
& everything had changed
towards art
ever since the arse of science
had fallen through as well,
let alone how politics
was still on the nose . . .

Then all the world's cattle
suddenly turned deathly ill
& no one could eat
any of the old swill anymore,
& all their gasses
were in the air everywhere
— all of them ticking off like time bombs
from the slightest spark!
Flesh was plague
& raining from the skies in those days!
And soon the same hell
befell swine as well,
& all the fishes of the seas were soured,
as all the fowl on top of it all . . .

The Hon. V. Q. Parnell
shipped out to the Middle East
on a quest to upgrade
the live exports of eels
& hares again,
— but was arrested on arrival in port
for not having a substantial moustache.
He soon escaped custody
& survived out in the Sinai desert
till the end of the spell
by chewing on the corner
of a thick De Chirico postcard
he swiped at a stall
out back of Tel–Aviv . . .

HELL'N

Drained away.
All strained away by the men.
Her pained face.
Blue,
she was,
this girl from Hell . . .

THE REGIONAL MAYOR

Out back of Hayrant,
in a corrugated shack
aside the plains,
the old mayor
was holed up in bed
with his albino concubine
— Iseult —
sucking out
through a pinhole in the shell,
the rich ripe yolk
of a free-range egg . . .

Suddenly he stopped & said:
"Baby, I can't live on this
fowl foetal juice no more."

Iseult asked him: *"Why not?*
I thought you liked it."

"I need a formed meat," he said.

Softly, she whispered:
"Well . . . I'm expectin', Dan."
(She wasn't — just wanted
to see how he'd react.)

He looked at her hard
like he'd just been turned to stone.

"You say that like it's mine."

"Well, who else would it be?"

"I only shoot blanks, love."

"'Fraid not."

"Like hell, you whore," he slurred.
"You're leavin' town."

She said nothing
& walked out of the bedroom
as he rang his chambers
to say he'd be late in again . . .

Iseult knew he'd be weighing up plans
to maybe get rid of her now,
& dump her out
in the desert somewhere
for the dingoes. . .

So later on
she shot him in an ear with his .22
as he shaved,
then chopped him up with a hatchet
& fed him to the hogs out back,
then dropped his bones
down an old mine shaft,
& out of sudden shame
suddenly hung herself
out in the barn . . .

And their funerals were very sad
& a small rural town ceremony
unfolded
& the local rag
lied of its excitement
— much to the desire
of its bored constituency.

15 BIRDS DREAM

15 birds with giant wings glide by.
In each beak is clutched a lie.
Sometimes they try to mate
with caged others
through panes of glass . . .

But these lies are small & unforgiveable
& they perpetuate the hate,
& when they fly by
the people sigh . . .

"No one's ever bled free in the sun.
On the cross was skill's name
for one & all,
& for all purpose."

In lieu of this though,
I propose a lake
for each bird to fly over
& cry on . . .

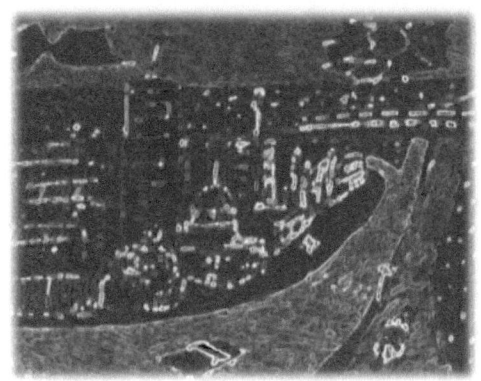

THE LEPERS OF FORTINBRAS

Cal had heard
— by local lore —
that Fortinbras was the place
where all souls born
defiled
were returned at their death
to acquire grace
before being recommissioned
to another spell on earth . . .

They all cluster
as a collective mass
of electrical vapors,
trapped atop the skinning tide
of the river Guille;

only after it rains
do they submerge,
compressed beneath the surface
as a solid
but undulating quilt,
& a buttress
to the singular filching of dragonflies,
which harrow them.
Nature there
abounds with unwitting clans
of all sorts
of returned eggs . . .

An old log bridge
lies between the mouth of Guille
& Fortinbras,
where only those given time to atone
are allowed to solely linger under
in the strange shadowed stillness
of the waters . . .

Nearby, the locals
pay for their eyes to be fixed
at Gateway Hospital,
out near where the bat colonies hang
in the giant berry trees
by the astrodome.

The sky of Fortinbras is fickle,
but forecasts are outlawed,
despite the town's penchant
for clairvoyance . . .

Down Unthanking Street
live 99 families,
each monitored by state-of-the-art
reconnaissance
for a TV game show.
Cal loves the girl in number 20.
Her name is Deja.
She has three mouths
— two above the nose —
still hungry for everything she sees
& savors,
& she clearly cares for people.
Cal plans to marry her one day.
Near everyone else hates her though,
but for Cal . . .

Her only friend is his enemy though.
Her name is Gaal.
She has the nine lives of a cat
& pretends to overlook
people's fetishes for time & fortune.
Cal has seen her denigrate Deja
before her own family.

She does it with a laugh,
because she's blind to the evil
in herself.
Deja sees Gaal the same
& only accepts the evil in her
when she herself is guilty
of a similar crime . . .

Cal met Deja
by way of reclaiming
the force of himself
through remonstration
at a public utility;
he'd entered an office
to accept a deposit back,
or the return of the same donation
he'd initially forfeited
— he can't remember —
but Deja was busy taking notes
at the time,
& Cal only ever noticed her
in the corner
because she sneezed,
& then he saw her eyes;
honeycomb crumbs lay plastered
across her lashes,
& when she blinked,
everything tumbled like dices
into her lap . . .

His heart gulped,
& he suddenly didn't care
why he was there anymore.
It was Spring
& she apparently
had a gag reflex to pollen
at the time.
He remembers
all he wanted to tell her
was the word *radula* . . .

She had natural mouths
used to smiling then.
They were initiatory.
Dead eyes passed by
& she breathed breath into them all.
All he remembers are her owl-like eyes,
& her animation,
& her warm smell;
milkish, but volcanic . . .

On his side though,
it's already completely lost on him.
The illusion is in their illusion.
It all soon turns sour after a while
when the mystery
is finally riven . . .

But it's all gone now.
Everywhere.
Everyone's buying everyone off now.
It's all $5.95 thanks.
With no class,
and no nous . . .

HE WHO LAUGHS WITH THE CROW

Left home
Walking fast
Tripping
Toppling
Getting up quick
Walking again
Adjusting my posture
Resuming my pace
Stepped in a puddle
Softly swore
Continued on
Eyes to the sky
A crow cawed WAHHHH
Laughed
Waited for traffic . . .

Crossed the road
Bird shat on my shoe
Loudly swore
Wiped if off against a tree
WAHHHH
Laughed again
Continued on
Reached a crossing
The light was red
Stopped.
Thought.
Wondered.
WAHHHH . . .

Amber flashed
Crossed without opinion
of the traffic
Placed my trust in green
Reached the other side
unharmed
Watched someone at a tram stop
Reached a group of shops
Glanced at windows
Stopped & stared in windows.
Sometimes to see products.
Sometimes to see myself.
Sometimes to look at the glass.

Continued on . . .

Spat once
One calf muscle began to ache
Changed my walking style
Did not stop
It seemed easier
Soon became fast as before
Reached the final roustabout
The light was red
Stopped again.
Waited at the lights.
Green popped
Continued on . . .

Passed the graveyard
Reached work
Tucked in my smile
Destroyed myself
Opened the door
Entered . . .

DONNA UNPLUGGED

In a lost world
of old, scolding days,
a young couple in a park
dared to openly kiss
& hug,
& all the sorry old bums
lain under the gums
screamed out in unison,
"Pig in, love!"

But time does its work,
& after years pass by,
the harder nights
soon dissipate
its sweet fervor
& flavors . . .

"Wedded . . ."
Donna scoffs to herself now,
"bedded . . .
bored . . .
an' beheaded,"
when dutifully frolicking
in her spouse's hold . . .

"It's beer . . .
On . . .
In . . .
Out . . .
Off . . .
And zzzzz again."

She soon wails
the old wives' woe again,
thinking love is too much pitied
when unsaid,
when not loved
in this lonely world.
It's the crime in hope's way
haunting all
to the what-not wicked ways of the world;
piecemeal,
like so much meat under glass,
as dropped in the pits
to the dogs . . .

What is there more to well for?
For all time's sake?
And at last forever?
What to part with now,
when all is gambled again on the world,
& still you lay alone
& long unloved?

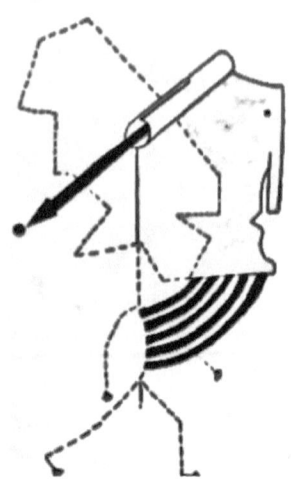

THAT ODD ID

Everyone seems to be
getting all tangled up
with what they overhear nowadays;
things that are one thing
sometimes turning
into another . . .

It's like everyone sees
the shadow first of what is,
before the is of what is isn't;
taking all these wild stabs
at what's secretly in back
of everything . . .

Like some hear
a boat as abort
or discussed as disgust
& guitar as gutter
& person as poison
& soil as soul
& sin as sing
& sperm as spam
or organise as agonise
& resource as racehorse
& ace-in-the-hole
is always asshole . . .

And like the old assume gag,
the therapist
means the rapist
or manslaughter
means man's laughter
& together
means to get her . . .

Or it's all retrograde in jumbles,
when evil becomes live
& god becomes dog
& nuclear becomes unclear
& kiss becomes sick
& funny becomes enough
& law becomes wall . . .

Everything in different rhythms
& emphasis,
like the way one takes a breath
in fight
or flight;
or the way a palate is formed
& sluggishly
takes to the tongue
in mixed accents . . .

Like the d dropped from devil
is always evil
& the o snatched from good
is always God,
& all the other
verbal sleights of hand
afforded;
like I did
is always the I.D.
done twice over
— the O.D. of the id —
that odd
done-in
id.

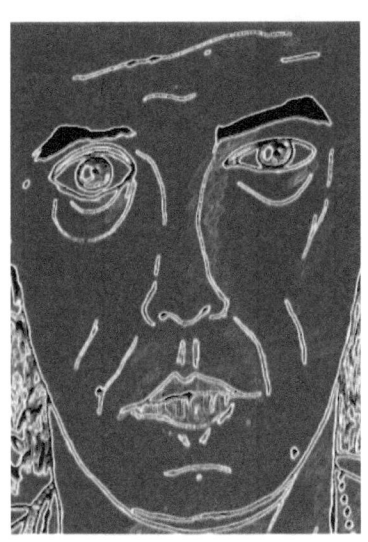

THIS DYSLEXIC DRANG

Restitution is an obvious goad.
He saw his mother die
from psyche bombs,
though his sisters
by less obvious crimes;
like the way a heart can be busted
just by crumbs . . .

One's seeds were just leaves,
& then sudden trees within moments;
their nested eyes
left like broken eggs
from the rush . . .

The whole family splintered
at the one end,
as like generations past.
Each brother lost
a certain inner balance
to hold the line.
But all those left behind
are still here,
& they'll laugh later on;
& anyone who feels like dying,
just doesn't . . .

"Psst.
This world is rotten.
Pass it on."

WAR DREAM
(France, 1944)

Walt had enlisted underage
& was soon shipped out
to the other side of the world
"on a lark."
They were in a five-way war
& they were all heading
into certain death . . .

All soldiers chose their texts
from the Bible as a shield
& walked out

into the battlefield
like blinded kids
& were shot to pieces.
But Walt was still alive,
& he felt like
he could still live forever . . .

Then the G.I. news came on
across the field-packs,
reporting how badly hit they were.
The shooting had lasted
for a full five hours.
Then the mangled body
of one of Walt's comrades beside him
vomited across his face,
& Walt was furious for some reason
— as if this was worse
than all the shooting! —
because he knew he'd have to move,
& it would probably be impossible,
& it would hurt . . .

It was all a bit *Gallipoli* in the end.
To be attached to a pennant
as a pimped-out hero for charity
in hometown Leongatha
was the only trench thought
he ever clung onto . . .

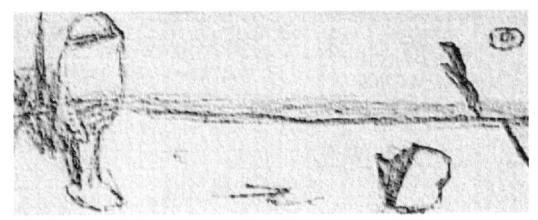

BETTER RED THAN WED

Back home,
still lead-headed from nuptial wine,
the neighbour's dogs howl
through the night
at the stray cats
rutting on the roof
next door . . .

STFU!

She married the wrong man.
Murdered
— I feel like lying low,
mulling over
all the dour reasons.
&#%@?!*#&^%$!
Nothing but the same old
dispiritations
as before;

just pegged out again
like a rag along a wire,
retched off
like a stinking corpse
to a marsh . . .

Sangfroid
these whittled hours now,
with the old busted moon
astride the pier;
& blooming
from the earth
in back,
the cicadas newly wailing,
like all those other dud
mandrakes of the mind,
with the damp sea air
in surround,
sitting there
like a stink
of the same old mould . . .

SEQUELAE

World whirr.
Moon burr . . .

Eons gone
like the ones unborn
will soon go . . .

An atrocity show
leaking sperm
to just start again . . .

Innocent,
till born dead . . .

HOONIO AND IOLA

So come the incurable
on *"Blessed Turtle Day"*
where the whys
& the wherefores
of each their sorry tales
are no longer of concern;
though the nurses watch on
from afar
just in case one runs amok . . .

No more of the old,
*"Step right up and see
the pickled brains of the damned
waxing dumb like clubbed does!"*
as before . . .

Their first look outside
at freedom
is like the wildest rain
— straight out
& unstoppable —
as if to meet glorious unknown rivers
that will never mouth
like sores again
at the end . . .

They stared wide-eyed
across the lush grounds
at all the streamers
& balloons
dancing free from asylum air.

But if all their woes,
each their gambled years
& wasted tears
cripple by as long before,
"Snatch them hardy,
their tartan shells"
— as the Matron coached them —
"and zoo them all!"

But the patients
weren't allowed to
"paw the amphibians,"

for the fear
they'd just be tossed
as grenades,
& could only watch on
as they hopped
& crawled about . . .

"All those squirming me and you's,"
Iola purred softly
in Hoonio's ear,
as they stood in the street
by the fence,
looking in
at where they met . . .

"Because you kissed me,"
he said.

She gently clasped his hand
& whispered even softer:
*"Just put them
in the tank
with the rest o' your rent."*
And for the first time ever,
Hoonio seemed to laugh freely,
as if finally
he did comprehend . . .

HOG HEAVEN

With *Sunday Morning*
blaring from the lounge
— drowning out
the neighbour's mower —
Gorma stood dreaming
at the kitchen window
out back,
in the morning sun,
with hungover eyes
& patchy memories
of the party
the night before,

half-listening to the bacon
cackling along
with the song
— his stomach growling
in accompaniment
like a blundering bass —
when the phone
began to *brrrr* . . .

*"Is that where ya hire
the long limos?"*
the caller asked.

Gorma loudly barked, *"Wha?"*

"Hire the long limos."

"Hide the wrong hippos where?"
he snapped back even louder.

But the caller heard
the thick barleyed tongue
lazily clacking
in Gorma's throat,
heard his gutter drawl,
sizing him up well,
knowing his education,
hearing his heavy blinks

78

— meat,
music
& guts
snarling in the b/g —
& he snickered
& hung up . . .

As Gorma assembled
his Sunday brunch,
he wondered again
about the sights
he might see
over the coming weeks
of his holidays;
like Wave Rock,
Monkey Mia,
the Pinnacles . . .

Later,
an old Frenchman rang
as Gorma bit into the pig.
He was applying
for the co-driver job
advertised
on the local store window
about the driving trip
Gorma was taking
around the land . . .

"I yam en eenternation-arl r-o-o-n-err,"
the caller declared,
and he said he'd come
"eighth in the interstate r-o-o-n,"
& that he'd *"lived in Mexico*
and Ar-shen-tina
and Colomb-wah
and Boliv-wah,"
& a few other places
where you can sprint . . .

Gorma said to him,
putting his sunglasses on:
"So why don't you RUN around
this country then?"

And he said,
"I'm too tired.
I w-e-e-r-n-t to see aborigines."

Gorma asked,
"You can drive ok then?"

But he said
"No, I can't drive."
He *could, "only r-o-o-n."*

Confused, Gorma snorted:
"Are you a surrealist?"
And the Frenchman barked,
"Cyclist? No."

Trying to stifle a laugh,
& with a blocked nose,
popping his ears
in the process,
Gorma suddenly spat hog
across the kitchen
at the portable TV
above the fridge,
hitting a newsreader
in the mouth,
who scratched his nose
as he talked about
a massacre . . .

FILCHER

The world,
it's said
— is said to be —
"A hell-bent factory,"
'cause everywhere
you love
& laugh
it kicks you in the knees;
it burns a hole
inside your heart,
your mind,
your soul,
your face;
it eats you up
& spits you out
& even takes
your cake.

THAT OLD FACTORY DREAM

Before the hurricane
she quickly grabbed him,
singing all her sweet little lies,
& he tried to love her,
but she'd cried
all those crimes . . .

VINCE

In a yellow house
a red-headed man in a hat
with 12 lit candles
around its brim
stabs his palette with a telescope,
squeezes out colours from the lens
& scrubs up
a million mornings
at once . . .

It's 4:00am.
Night is in its throes.
Soon, a typical sentence of light
will burn across
the fields of corn,
& a typical day will evolve
& the insects will buzz by
& the birds will sing out
& the folk of Arles
will plough the crops
with the bray of nags
at their toes,
whilst Vince stabs it all down
with coagulating blood
into the canvas;

one after another,
a few a day
in the scorching sun . . .

Bashed & beaten
by the mistral winds
that swirls & careens
& knocks him down
like fists & thunderbolts,
he'll get up again & again
like a man in the ring
armed with only his imagination . . .

His brushes are zinc guns,
firing off poplars & horizons;
loading & reloading,
burning up the night
with translucent hues
& luminescent shadows . . .

His singing brushes are thrush quails
burrowed in hutches,
incubating eggs,
watching not for tomorrow,
but for tomorrow's tomorrow
where there are lost souls
worse than he,
in epileptic convulsions

from pollution,
& disease;
where to even walk is unsafe;
where atrocities of all sorts
come in at all sides;
where men & women
both in their subterranean worlds
skin their shins
& shed their skins
just to exist intact;
where lies
are the only exchanging currencies;
where people are stabbed
in their sleep;
where children are slaughtered
on the news;
where people kill
to be noticed . . .

And these people
come back to Arles
a century back,
to the yellow house,
& the glowing man
under candlelight,
not just to laud him,
but to keep those wicks alight.
And they said he was *mad* . . .

FLOSSING RIBS
SO THE HEART MIGHT SEE

The icy moon
roving the same,
seemed as shamed . . .

G-d, the old juniper tree vanished
like a haunting face
as all the town locals
ran past it
on tippy-toes
all over the place,
past the tracking-stations
dotting the cliffs,

in the search for more
muddied mirrors
in which to preen
for sense . . .

All the eggheads
could hear inside
was the clatter
of other worlds in back,
like a bad rig's failing rear springs.
The quiet had been smashed
yet again
by the same old
incomprehensible phenomena
of calamity
that always invades
everything around here
in the end . . .

The Postman:
"The fickleness
with which each soul
gruelly bustles
from the gloom!"

The Bookseller:
"The hooded fatalism
with which each is felled!"

The Lollipop Lady:
"Granite brains,
granite thoughts,
one and all!"

The Dogwalker:
"To the bones,
the frigging gangrening marrow!"

The Jogger:
"All of us mashed up again
like once at the chugging egg!
The worms afossicking!"

The Madame:
"The muted fumbles
and Anglicised cheer
of each in check,
to be all so ever less evolved!"

The Publican:
"Just to grievously know that,
all along,
no matter
how much headway
is ever made,
all is crud!"

The Town Biddy:
"The finale always comes,
hungry as it goes,
creeping upon
each hoodwinked dupe
as all!"

The Lighthouse Keeper:
"In the end,
what is inherently worse,
a God without teeth
or a God without eyes?"

The Old-Time Angler:
"The atrocities
of what we've all
witnessed!"

His Parrot Wife:
"You mean,
of what we've all
so soberly endorsed!"

The Local Priest:
"But,
for the others to come,
still wrapped up
in their sickly hymens!"

His Housekeeper:

"And catching all the dregs
of each stilted act!"

The Taxidermist:

"Distributing the same old
sealed holocausts of old!"

The Horse Doctor:

"They've all duly taken
their sodden oats in time
to ceremoniously recompose
one and all!"

The Barber:

"Here again,
in the same old
beachy-bleached texture and hue,
fully-fleshed or sans!"

The Corrupt MP:

"The green, multifarious jostlings
of what properties attract
and repulse!"

The Town Bike:

"The finicky aspects
that infer one soul to another
from jellybacked road to road!"

The Town Lush:
"All of us drenched
in the same old sweaty rags
from centuries
of long-soured
dour tuitions!"

The same tree
faintly appeared again
like a daunting face;
the failing sun
setting the same,
forlorn as love
at rest . . .

CREASE OF A WING

She vanished with my cross;
homespun girl
puffing cigars by the sea.
The bloody stars of dusk
— *let me in.*

FRIEND OR FIEND DREAM

There was a dog barking.
No, it was a cat
being punished by Dreck,
who was savagely beating it
till it turned into Allie's's dog.
But no matter how much
I pleaded to stop beating it,
the cat was all screams.
It's nose was frightening.
But it overcame it,
& turned into
this little shaggy terrier.
I think it even wore clothes.
And I think Gracie was there.
We were all sitting on the bed
in Dreck's room
in Larco Street.
I was terrified
of this cat-turned-dog
trying to jump up on the bed.
But as it did,
& was calmed,
Dreck left and I woke . . .

AND THE DEAD SHEEP
WASH UP ON SHORE

Wan Louie La Salle
gravely nodded to the court
as his lawyer announced
he was professor of chemistry
& dean of the science department
at ███████████ University
in Australia,
& how he had become
addicted to ice
over a *"slow assassination
of the heart"* . . .

The lawyer told the court
that the affair
had *"gone on for years,"*
& that initially Louie had found
farming products
in his wife's rusty jeep,
& later
tickets to sheepdog trials,
& scrawled study notes
from an agricultural lecture
at the same university
where her lover taught
as professor of horticulture . . .

She herself was professor of biology
in the same science block,
& Louie soon suspected
her new regard to fabrics
& her sudden sensual need for wool,
ever since beefcake ex-shearer,
Porto Royo,
had arrived on the faculty
from the bush,
out back of Yarma . . .

Louie had followed her for a time
when she was out & about,
& would check her phone records
when he could;

but she was always surgically clean
with her moves,
& impeccably precise
with the history of her calls . . .

It frustrated him no end
for many years.
He'd become an alcoholic
because of all the trauma
& all the eggshell-walking
around work;
but his deterioration was swift,
becoming consumed with jealousy
& paranoia.
His cuckoldry was long
the scuttlebutt
across campus . . .

He became more obsessed
as time went on.
He soon swabbed his wife
as she slept
& had everything analyzed
back at his lab in class.
Then he stripped her brush of hair
& had it beamed.
Soon, he was siphoning pipes
for a cup of her water.

Then slitting her throat
for a glimpse of her blood.
Everything sank in her;
his heart in her,
his seed in her,
his tears on her dress . . .

"She held it all,
but gave it no sanction!"
he pleaded to the jury.
"She dismissed
the entire gambit of my heart!"

They were both
calm of mind enough
in the course of their marriage
not to have children;
calm enough
to establish the growth
of "*lies and torment.*"
They both lied at large,
as though there was no mud
on their souls
— but he caught the first pang;
he peeled the first scab.
She caught him snooping once,
but gave him mercy.
That was when he knew
he was food;

"Old food,
eaten,
processed,
and
shitted out
in lumps of laughter."

His last words screamed
to the jurors
as he was dragged from the dock
by guards
were in broken French:
"Il ya a toujours une femme
qui pourrit votre ame a la boue!"*

*["There's always one woman
who rots your soul to slush!"]

THE ENDING DAY

The lust of all; gone at last.
The old axes & logs
& all the parlayed eggs
& the faltered bonds
& the blundered dregs
& the silted ponds.
All now s   t   i   l   l
and gone . . .

That simple truth,
with all the old ghosts
still inside,
aside the creaks,
each busted eye,
each dunking toe,
& every hocked o'clock
the same old deathly write-off . . .

All closing now to the light,
all the old hoary ha's,
& the curt regrets
for everything long passed,
just or unjust,
with the squeaking wheels
to the rows of stones . . .

THE HEART IS A GORGON

With thunder thighs
& bitching eyes,
she stormed into his life
like something nuclear . . .

With a heart of fool's gold
she stole his ragged soul,
with a face
like an elephant's sphincter . . .

"O God,
let go of my heart, darlin'!
You're eating the meat away
like a size 20 caterpillar!"

But she's not fooled
by a single protest;
she knows her spousal rights
go with the territory . . .

She's a predator
on the march,
leaving his shell
for landfill . . .

For years
he'd howled at the moon
like a lonely hound
baying for company . . .

He'd cruised the world
like a famished shark
itching for something
to gnaw on . . .

He'd smashed
into a thousand panes
like a deluded bird,

thinking he saw
a prospective partner;
& all he ever found
was disillusion
& indifference . . .

And then up she came
out of the horizon
like a mushroom cloud
engulfing him.
And here he lies now,
in a mangled pile
of hips & elbows,
bereft of spine, guts, & sinews,
with her burping him back
in his face,
& laughing down
great spitted chunks
of his undissolvable secrets,
plucking his lashes
one by one, saying:
"He loves me,
he loves me not,"
like a twisted dolt
in a country meadow
demolishing the final daisy . . .

1994

MAGGOT DAWN MANNA

Another comedian has died;
another old seal gone on celluloid.
They're all dropping
like gassed birds nowadays.
It seems like the source
of every jibe has dried up
like a mottled well
& strangled them all.
They've smashed the millionth waterhole
& finally wailed.
Or it's like everything
has been skinned
& they've all left
to quilt the scab . . .

It'll take a long time
for each weal to heal
from all these woes though.
First, there has to be the soak.
Then salt's sprinkled
across the top,
before being rolled over
in the shards,
till it's all just vinegared good,
& pickled sour
as a festered truth.
It's only then
that it'll be plucked out
& praised,
redeemed as fodder
for the new crank's lash
& all their double breaths
again . . .

So another comedian is dead.
Another million gasps have gone.
Another million frowns
have tucked in
another notch
around the skull,
like a trusty tourniquet
squeezed on the skinning arm
of Death . . .

They'll soon make hay
of his gifted muse
& refashion it
as a hasty starch,
then colour it all up
with a doctored face,
so they can all wander about
in their zombie herds
in masks,
chewing soothed
with knowing,
like a holy donut
in a marshal's hand . . .

A SCALPEL IN THE TOSS
AS BALLOONS FLOAT ABOUT

Extrude,
divest your museum,
you irrational sick terror
of a patriot!

The ingredients of your perfection
grate me.
It lap-wings,
mesmerizes you like a dodo!

The cavalry of angels
at your banquet
talk with the evil whisper
of zephyrs!

DRAG ME, AIM ME

Well, it's all been done.
The corner's been cornered
& the conning's been conned.
You can feel it all
welling up now,
like the whole world's
about to blow.
You can smell it . . .

Now, the big trick's not to disavow it.
Yeah sure, you think
you've got cherries to spare
at the end
— but who's got the tree?
♫ *She bought it,*
but she aint gonna use it. ♫

It's all been stamped out
by those others on the march.
But if the scheme goes stymied
once more,
it'll all just pass on
to the next unsorry soul,
or the next transfigured world.
You well & truly know that . . .

I don't know any dogs
that are "Best Friends" to anyone.
All they do is lounge about
& feed on your love
like ghouls, I'm told.
But I'm cynical now,
because it's back
to lonesomeness again.
And old memories of someone
to hold onto again?
No fucking fear . . .

An old toxic she
probably still thinks
she couldn't find a fly
to take to her flesh like me,
or even a worm
to her old jellied bones.
She couldn't be more wrong . . .

Soon enough
we'll both be dumped
under the trash anyway,
like old mottled chunks
of yellow cake
not even the daemons of the hereafter
would sourly burrow up
to taste . . .

So it's lost time all the way;
& for the ether
that's all there is anyway.
It's a no either/or anathema
for all or nothing.
Nothing but the mis-glory
of being long
misunderstood,
in spite of it . . .

THE SCRUBBING END

He suddenly left
because he was having trouble
laughing there.
It just wasn't welcome anymore.
Joy went out the window
& everyone just ended up
coughing at each other
all the time . . .

"I'm leaving."

"Where are you going?"

"I don't know.
I don't care.
Anywhere from here.
I want to laugh freely.
I don't want to have to rehearse."

TO ASSESS THE SINS
OF ALL ASSASSINS

"We have lashed you to this chair
for good reason.
Before you is a screen;
the screen of your new mind.
You shall infiltrate yourself now,
without discrimination
as before,
& take to yourself

the frivolous concerns
of fictitious others
that will now long rule your days,
in the misbegotten way
your systems have long
subconsciously responded
in emotive manners
to all those events of life
that ARE real
& not ever fictitious,
& everything that is daily concocted
in timeless truths
will now jockey
your every thought & act.
Everything that is told to you
today
will NOW be your telling.
Everything that is shown to you
today
will NOW be your doing.
You will soon be dispatched
to the tropics
where disease is rampant;
but we will equip you with
medicines as appropriate.
Here, swallow these placebos
for practice.

Load it, Buz . . .

See the horrible newsman.
But the gentle weatherwoman.
Swallow . . .

Old black & white films.
New colourful game shows.
Which is better?
Swallow . . .

Idiots & heroes.
Idiots & heroes.
See how they run?
Swallow . . .

Who did what where & when?
Gulp it all down as shown.
Let it all slowly dissolve
in the little plexus
of your belly.
Swallow . . .

Don't you like that quirky tale
about soap?
Swallow . . .

Look at the glory & majesty
of those worm-pills for mutts!
Swallow . . .

Don't you like this cardboard candidate
& all that he promises?
Swallow . . .

He uses the very same shampoo as you.
He feeds his pooch
the very same dried niblets
you feed your own.
Swallow . . .

Don't the analysts
seem to accentuate
your very own concerns about policy?
Swallow . . .

Now, time for a little tale
about potato chips.
Swallow . . .

Oh, see how flakes of wheat
slowly fall into the bowl
like snippets of the sun
raining onto the earth?
Swallow . . .

116

Mmm. Fizzy cola.
The sweet black nectar.
Swallow . . .

Here is another candidate.
Your candidate's very adversary.
Swallow . . .

Aren't his eyes too close together?
Is he not too short
to lead a whole people,
an entire modern civilisation?
Swallow . . .

He likes the fish-spread you hate.
He wears that stinky aftershave
you know is wrong.
Swallow . . .

In time,
you will grow to hate him
& all that for which he stands.
Swallow . . .

One day you will wish to purchase
a cantaloupe,
& we will help fulfil this wish of yours.
Swallow . . .

You will sit by coastal towers
& wait for us to call you.
Swallow . . .

You love to hear my voice now.
You cannot function properly
without hearing
the timbre of its rich soft purr.
Swallow . . ."

A SUCCUBUS SNEERS
ON A BROKEN MAN'S BACK
AS HE SNORES

"With fastened eyes
you sprinkle your spice
malignant man
into our salty skunk wads;
a jellied conch imbued
with the slip of a berry.
Go on sleuth,
answer the Orphic minx
who purrs grandeur
across your heart,
who teases fears
into forged guns,
who curdles spoonfuls of dust
into the zillion eyes
of a bustling, sloshed battalion
of burping,
window-dressed ogres
with tiny teeth
g-n-a-s-h-i-n-g . . ."

EVERYTHING STARTS WITH A STING

Amoeba man chases sparks
of flashing fireflies in the dark;
snapping twigs,
screaming falls,
hunting larks . . .

Owl claws gleam,
drowning mice,
as bats swoop by
sounding crickets out;

120

pinging rocks with beams,
splitting silence
with sudden wings . . .

Amoeba man sings out a song
as mosquitoes quell
the depths of his blood . . .

Skin sores soon evolve
in amoeba man,
pitching his bones to dust . . .

Soon, cancered clans
knock hard in his wives;
fingers thaw to hatch
as elbows nudge
to escape the rite . . .

Batting eyes revolve
to soon see all things
named as such;
buildings rising like waves,
machines caterwauling
like stricken beasts
at large . . .

LOST IN THE RUBBLE

Fish up that bail
and hail it down like rain!
Avalanche the whole fucking thing!
Pick up a club and shatter it
into a million fragments!
Grind it into the earth,
and it's home:
not as a migrant . . .
a refugee . . .
an alien . . .
but a basic slave . . .
a groveling lackey
to love!

SKINT ON SKINS

Lonely Laarp has not made love
for years now,
& even then the last time
was with an escort;
but it wasn't enjoyable at all,
because he felt a little sick
by the heavy scent
on her breath.
Though it's only now
he recalls
that he didn't really care about it
too much at the time
because he'd desperately
tried to kiss her . . .

He's got a feeling now
that he was more upset
by her refusal
to kiss him back
than by her putrid breath.
But he was repugnant himself!
It's only later
you make up
all these moral excuses . . .

Laarp has not fucked a thing
for the last five years
but his mind.
Each night he drunkenly
nuzzles down deep
into the mattress,
writhing in the same old
faintly preserved trench
of his ex-wife
— as if still sprawled
on her belly —
hacking his unwanted hips
into the springs,
in the same old ghostly *boing* of lore.
But sometimes
he feels like he's just a loner bear
trying to bury itself down deeper
into the winter mud
to disappear forever . . .

He sees
all these teasing beauties in movies
& magazines everywhere,
on billboards
& the sides of trams,
grinning gloriously happy,
with even white teeth
shimmering like shells,

124

& polished skin clean as snow
& their fearless eyes
staring out clear as ice,
& he can see everything in them,
the history of the whole cruel world
reflected back at him
like they're from the sockets of G-d
damning one & all . . .

He's never met a model,
but they keep imbuing themselves
to make him wish
that one day he could.
But, see,
he's got green buck teeth
& facial scars
& early greying hair in a fizzing halo
& jug-handles for ears,
not to mention
his "damaged" personality
forever on display . . .

And he gets this gnawing pain
inside himself
that won't ever leave,
because he knows
that he'll never interest a beauty
like any of those

shoved down his throat
night & day,
because he just doesn't appear right,
or together,
like them . . .

It doesn't matter
that he sometimes thinks
that he thinks for himself,
or he's got all these original views,
or that
he's almost cellularly pure now
— because nothing
is being used;
it's like he's almost
re-virginised himself now
because of the lack of use —
& it doesn't matter
that he's got enough buckets of love
inside himself
to fill a dam,
or that he would only ever
harm a fly . . .

He knows at heart
he's only a wetback to the dream
like billions of others.
He's only a sucker to the sham
that's hoodwinked all.

So he doesn't love anyone.
And no one loves him.
But it's more than that now.
He doesn't know if it's just him,
but he feels more & more
like everyone is slowly being
sequestered from one another
— not to mention
from themselves —
that everyone is just slowly
isolating themselves
& losing touch
with what they all inherently are,
or once were . . .

Though, he realises
this could just be him
& not everyone else at all,
as he's trying not to generalise anymore,
because, when he gets down to it
he knows
that he really doesn't know anyone,
& he knows
that he shouldn't delude himself anymore
into thinking that he does.
No one knows anyone.
Even though, at bottom,
they're all the same,

& he often wonders about
the whole bloody thing.
But, it's like,
soon as he mentions *"The Soul"* to anyone
these weirding days
they just laugh in his face
as if he's mad, sad,
old-fashioned
& insane . . .

"Maybe they always did,"
he thinks.
*"Maybe they always have
and always will."*
He doesn't know anymore.
"Maybe they're right too,"
he ponders . . .

In truth, the word "soul"
has never made much concrete sense
to him anyway.
Even though he's long tried
to pretend to himself
that it does,
because it seems to capture
a feeling,
a sense of knowing,
& he sometimes wonders
if that's it?

128

"But really, what is it?"
he always asks himself . . .

He can't count
how many encyclopedias
he's thumbed over the years;
how many *Gray's Anatomies*
he's foraged through
to find this thing
on the body's map . . .

He once rang
The Royal College of Surgeons
& asked the most prized quacks,
but not one could ever clear it up.
They've found nothing
but rotted gizzards inside all:
a meat that rots.
"It's an imaginary organ,"
they all told him.
"You're looking for
the phantom gland of faith."

The only place he's ever found it in
is the dictionary,
& even then he could feel
old Sammy Johnson
nudging him in the ribs
with a little scoff . . .

"What do I do?"
he asks himself all the time
as he tries to sleep in the staddle.
Does he stick to this
"maybe" truth,
that there's something more to life;
or just go hook for crook
for the sensual pleasures
of the bones
till he's dead
like everyone else?
It's just that all those porcelain faces
shoved in his eyes everywhere
leave him completely empty now.
They just stare through him
as they vainly pose
with their bored Vogued grins . . .

And then he thought,
"Hell, maybe I'm queer."
But then he laughed that one off,
because, Christ, men make him
even more sick in the guts.
"Just look at me,"
he says disgustedly to himself
in a public glass:
*"Could I ever take me home
and have myself off?"*

So he keeps going back
to all those other distractions
that used to keep him levelled
when he was young,
like music,
good ol' reliable song;
but there's only seven notes
that can be juggled,
& all that's beginning
to bore him now as well . . .

It's the same with art, too.
There's only a basic handful of colours
to ever see him through.
*"Music?"*he snarls to himself now,
"What the hell is sound anyway?
And art?
What does it do in the long run?"
Questioning everything.
Valuing it all.
Haggling with himself . . .

"And sex?
Genitals are the most primitive things!"
he rants at himself.
"The whole body
with all its stupid buttons
and pumps!"

He thinks that some people
riddled with despair at a young age
suddenly break an unseen veil
& it's very hard
to ever see anything as beautiful again
without that maul anymore.
He sometimes thinks he knows
what the solution to all this is though,
but he doesn't want to
resort to that either . . .

"There must be something
worthwhile to do
to have to keep taking
all these idiot breaths,"
he seethes to himself alone in bed.
So, he doesn't fuck,
doesn't do anything;
because he can't fuck,
can't do anything . . .

He sometimes wonders
if anyone feels the same way as him
all the time,
forever & a day.
He once thought
it was all just a phase,
but it's just rolled on & on
for an eternity now . . .

He used to always think
there was a G-d
& sometimes he thinks there still is,
but often he can't help
but ruminate over the fact
that if that's the case
then the whole world mess at bottom
is His,
& that at heart
He must be as thick as man,
being clad in the same image
& all that . . .

"Yeah, sure, He's inventive,"
he says to himself,
"But the whole thing's just dumb!"
And the simple fact
that everyone is
— inherently —
constantly hurt inside,
no matter how many
cover it up so well
— & sometimes he thinks
that's all everyone is here to learn;
that everyone just has to learn
how to conceal
all this hurt —
is unforgivable to him . . .

He can admire G-d for His talent,
but not His cruelty,
because it just seems like
everyone means nothing,
& he often ponders over that;
that maybe G-d is just like everyone too,
that G-d feels as if
He means nothing as well . . .

Laarp often ponders over the feeling
that maybe G-d doesn't know
what He's doing either,
that He never has & never will,
that G-d doesn't know why
He's here either,
or what to do . . .

He drunkenly wonders,
as he snuggles down
into the shallow staddle
of his lost wife's heft,
how long it's been
since G-d last made love?
"What have we got to do . . ."
he fumes into the pillow,
kicking his feet,
   *". . . hitch to the slaughterhouse
to get a simple rut?"*

ENFRANCHISED PARVIS

When I first met her eyes,
she was lying in wait
for the Reaper
with his scythe
& then she died
. . . in a body-bag,
& they carried her away.

And now the hollow *"ha"*
of people chuckling,
the birds whispering on
their song,
& all their talk of money
leaves me
just as cold for love . . .

And then I tagged along
to see them bury her,
& they lowered her in the hole,
& the diggers
just slowly filled it in,
& then it came screaming out
. . . her soul!

"I want to thank you
for coming to see me off.
You're the only one to show.
I don't know why
I killed myself.
Or why I killed them all
as well."

When I last met her eyes
she was flying away,
with an angel
at each side,
& then I cried
. . . onto her grave,
as they carried her away.

1992

DIASTOLE AND SYSTOLE

I hate you
& everything you stand for.
I despise your dogeared states
of security
& respectability.
I pray that one day
you will lose everything
& that you will have no choice
but to tunnel
within yourself
in the desperate search
to find some form of substance
as a reason to resume . . .

I love you
& everything you can't hide behind.
I adore your fickle quirks
of sadness
& inability.
I fear that one day
you will gain everything
& that you will dumbly
succumb
to the arms of society,
with the desperate longing

to escape
from such a natural
chaotic reality
given everyone;
& I hope that your organs fail
one by one,
& that you wholly cherish
it all
as you perish;
& I beg the Reaper
that you die
the most glorious private death
unknown to anyone;
& I pray
that you will be born again
as the exact same
atrocity
you've always been . . .

THE WEDDING AXE

Old jilted Rogan is so sick
of this waiting-room condition;
being stuck at home all the time
since being retrenched
from his government job.
And now the car's shot
& he's flat broke
& the cupboards are bare
& the soles of his shoes
are as thin as a Tally-Ho's . . .

The whole thing's
toying with his mind.
He can hear all these ghosts

biting their nails
up in the attic.
He thought he caught one
dry-heaving
in the kitchen sink
the other night.
And now the walls
are turning to flesh
& the doorjambs to bones
& the drapes
to withered husks of skin
as the carpet ripples out
like ponds of blood
throughout the house
as he lonely sobs . . .

Sometimes he listens
sceptically
to shock jocks
sneering across the waves
that
"chickens are all full o' milk now"
& *"cans o' beans
are all really eggs"*
& *"everyone's riding crocodiles
 down the main street of town"*
when
— more often than not —

as cabin fever
really kicks in at night
when he feels most exposed,
he can't doubt
what they're saying
might just be right
all along . . .

His state-appointed therapist,
Dr. Krasche,
tells Rogan that he suffers
from a form of drapetomania
— a morbid desire
for freedom at any cost.
But all Rogan knows is,
if he hadn't found
that old battered uke
of an old flame's
out in the garage,
he would've given up the ghost long ago.
Just one strummed chord alone
can sometimes save the day . . .

In his heart of hearts,
he sees all this woundedness
that's around
— often wrongly defined
as a by-product of money,

or the lack thereof —
as more a consequence
of the impermeable lack
of inquisitiveness in people
to create a tune.
He's always deemed pianos
the only mechanisms
able to truly soothe
the brutalities of life . . .

Years ago,
he used to go down
to The Monday Club across town,
where they'd all sit around
on old piano stools
& just tinkle away
on rows of ancient German uprights
as they talked
& laughed
& drank home-brewed beer
over the hours,
creating such amateurish dins
as the night unfolded,
that would always gel
into a soaring cacophony
of wild drunken riffs
that would inspire
such incredible joys

& sorrows
in everyone
before they all headed home . . .

But then,
one night,
all the old ex-con tuners turned up
& to pass the time between repairs
they all sat back
and poured metho from their flasks
& sniffed at bags of glue
& smoked ice
& staggered around like maniacs
everywhere,
trying to bite the walls,
& grinding themselves into the doors,
which spooked everyone.
And that was the end
of The Monday Club . . .

For the last nine years
Rogan had worked in the deli
at the National Space Office,
out on the edge
of the Jelungulu salt pans.
Ms. Lilli Garmbay
— the director of the facility —
had instilled in her staff

a strict regime of calisthenics
to follow,
& they'd all just hand
themselves over
to government quacks
each dawn,
so they could inject them
with the urine of pregnant women;
which they promised
would help tone them all up,
& tune them all in,
just like old Mario Lanza
used to do
to keep his adenoids in check
& help deflect *"corruption"*
from the natural timbre
of his *"gift"* . . .

As they'd all do jump-ups
& sit-ups
out in the car park
by the rows of white radomes
pointed to the heavens,
they'd all vaguely intone
as a parroting chorus
the woolly redacted mantra
of their boss's eclectic creed
in code . . .

"Binko hee,
Binko har,
Binko
Yar yar yar yar yar,
Dah dah dah dah,
Dah dah dah
. . . along."

At day's end,
the company would instill
in them all
certain mind-controlled
security measures . . .

They'd strap them down
in rubber chairs,
& they'd each succumb
to the indoctrination
of specific government
"*hush kits*"
by a dour technician
of the highest clearance
deemed *"The G-d Ranger"* . . .

What he would do
was coined *"The G-d Act"*
by decree,
to keep them all unaware

of what it was
they were all really doing
for a living,
so as to secure the base
& keep them all
from spilling the beans
to the outside world
about what was being developed
below ground . . .

In lieu of any sort of personal life,
Ms. Garmbay would "*marry*"
each of them off
— in a Pavlovian sense —
to certain industrial machines
on the lower floors;
& she'd promise
that come each
their Silver Anniversary there,
after a lifetime of work,
they would each be entrusted
with an implement
— "*a cyber axe*" —
that would enable them
to "*divorce*" themselves
from the procedure
they were initially coerced
to endure,

"as a sacrifice to their nation,"
so as to one day
be able to return
to the outside world,
and resume some form
of a *"normal"* civilian life
in their dwindling years;
goading them all on
with the notion
of that one *"glorious day"*
they could all take to
— again —
the natural rites of passage
given everyone . . .

ANGEL IN THE AIRPORT

Angel shoes
seal angel toes.
See angel soles
haply stamping
out snails?

Angel baby gapes through the pane,
watching planes climbing high,
balloons floating by,
birds gliding past,
apples falling down . . .

Angel baby slips,
suddenly thudding to the floor,
breaking its wrist-like neck;
its mouth a kiss on floor,
vomiting up shells . . .

Tourists file by,
tangling themselves in the laces
of its untied booties;
lynching themselves up
in knots everywhere . . .

Is this what happens
when angels forget?
Is this what happens
when angels are met?

LATE REQUIEM FOR A BYSTANDER

"Low scunging I,
Gulbak Glanner,
now of the earth's deep inner mud
legally will
to allow righteous Death,
through a scribe,
to bespeak through me
this gone umpteenth year
of my unjust passing.
X."

Contemptuous,
he lays doubly fostered.
(Why they all wee the why's woe?)
Brie, his lump of love,
still lies beneath
the stone's green.
She'd buttressed him once
— her long lashes
shielding his calm for a spell —
but because of that
there is not yet her hole,
but ironically,
long his . . .

He began as wronged
& was long thrashed for it;
by that time though,
he was already
transmogrified . . .

PROPERTIES
In an eye: two festered hills.
In the tubes: a stringed web of glue.
The mouth: a searing wick.
Across the gap: the blundered ban.
And in the centre: a piece of glass.

He only ever long dreamt
of bouncing balls
off the corners of ceilings.
He once crowed for romance.
His blunted eyes recorded;
each lens a weary weir
on second glance . . .

Old Liona danced wearily
across his grave
as she promised,
when once she breathed in him
stolen fires
— but she got him wrong
again —
& after that

it's all just war
& bones
& busted faces anyway,
with all the boots back on
to be marched again.
Skip his last mile.
That's the crater.
That's the bomb.
☠